II Cor. 8:21

THE OKAPICAT
AN *Audrey Amaka* STORY

WRITTEN and ILLUSTRATED BY

BRENT VERNON

ISBN 978-0-9831638-2-4   Visit us online at *WWW.BRENTVERNON.COM*

"That does it!" grumbled Audrey Amaka, wadding up another piece of paper and tossing it over her shoulder. "My handwriting is awful!" Audrey was leaning against the big fig tree in her back yard.

"Maybe if you would practice more often—" called Mrs. Amaka from inside the house.

"I *am* practicing, Mom!" Audrey whined.

"Not enough, apparently," said Mrs. Amaka. "Your father and I expect you to do your best, Audrey. We have seen *much* better penmanship from you!"

That was true. At the last parent-teacher conference, Miss Nell told the Amakas that Audrey's handwriting had become sloppy. '*Terribly sloppy*' were the teacher's words.

"It takes too much time," Audrey sulked. "Good handwriting is a lost art. And I'm okay with that."

"What matters now is that you follow instructions," said her mother, "and be sure to clean up the mess you're making!"

Just as Audrey was about to apologize for her bad attitude, the doorbell rang.

DING-DONG!

"That's probably the boys!" Audrey whooped and ran into the house.

Audrey opened the front door expecting to see her best friends Nelson and Doodle. To her surprise, a young okapi* was standing on the welcome mat with a silly grin on her face. An okapi is a member of the giraffe family, but Audrey had never met one.

"I'm *here!*" announced the little lady.

"I see that," said Audrey, feeling confused and annoyed.

"And *you're* here!" said the okapi. "It's you! It's really YOU... neckless Cousin Audrey!" She lunged at Audrey and gave her a big hug.

Audrey quickly pulled away and took a few steps back.

"Well, who do we have here?" asked Mrs. Amaka as she entered the room.

"Oh me!" said a familiar gravelly voice. "I hope this letter isn't too late!"

They all looked up to see Mr. Weaver swoop through the doorway and land on the kitchen table.

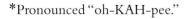

"Letter? What letter?" asked Audrey.

"*This* letter," said Mr. Weaver. He pulled an envelope out of his backpack and handed it to her.

Audrey opened the envelope, unfolded the letter, and started to read.

6

Our Beloved Cousins,

Since the day we heard of Audrey's bravery in the Black Mamba episode, our youngest daughter has been asking to meet her.

My wife and I will be out of the country for several days. We are allowing our daughter, Ornela, to stay with you while we are away. I'm sure you won't mind. She is a wonderful girl.

Ornela will arrive at your home on Monday afternoon and return to Congo by riverboat one week later.

Sincerely,

Jules

Jules Kayembe* (an Okapi relation)

"It was nice of them to ask," Audrey said sarcastically. "Are they *really* related to us, Mom?"

Mrs. Amaka gave her a stern look, then turned to Ornela. "We have always loved Cousin Jules," she said with a smile. "And you have your father's eyes. *Of course* you are welcome to stay with us!"

Mr. Weaver let out a sigh of relief. Audrey bit her lip.

*Ornela's last name is pronounced "ky-EM-bee."   7

When Mr. Amaka came home, he was delighted to meet Ornela and suggested that they celebrate her arrival with a trip to The OssiCone, the best ice cream shop in town.

"I love this place!" said Audrey as they entered the shop. "I always get three scoops of jackalberry nutgut."

"If that's your favorite," said Ornela, "it'll be *my* favorite too!"

8

　　While they were eating, Audrey noticed that Ornela was watching her intently.

　　"Aren't you gonna eat your ice cream?" Audrey asked.

　　"I *still* can't believe I'm here with my famous cousin Audrey!" Ornela blurted. "When I heard how brave you were with those mean ol' snakes, I decided to be brave too—just like you!"

9

"You don't have to be just like me," said Audrey.

"Well, you're smart too," Ornela continued. "You're the best at every subject in school!"

"That's not completely true," Audrey gulped, thinking about her sloppy handwriting.

"But that's what I heard!" said Ornela. "And guess what. I'm gonna be as smart as you someday!"

The sun was setting as they left The OssiCone. Ornela had not stopped talking. Just as Audrey's mind was beginning to wander, she heard her cousin ask a very disturbing question.

"Did you notice *MY* blue shoes, Cousin Audrey?"

Audrey stopped in her tracks. She looked down and gasped.

"Check 'em out!" Ornela beamed. "Blue shoes—just like yours!"

Audrey wanted to scream. She took great pride in the sparkly blue high heels her parents had given her. But sure enough, Ornela was also wearing a very fashionable pair of sparkly blue shoes!

"They aren't *a lot like* mine," Audrey snapped. "My shoes have more sparkles and higher heels."

"But mine can do *this!*" Ornela said, clicking her heels together. Suddenly, her shoes lit up with a hundred twinkling lights.

Just as suddenly, Audrey realized that it was going to be a *very* long week.

The next morning, Ornela asked if she could go to school with Audrey. Audrey gritted her teeth and agreed. At recess, she took Ornela to meet Nelson and Doodle on the playground.

When Audrey spotted the boys, she noticed that something was wrong with Nelson's ears. She also noticed that Doodle, who usually wore a bright smile, wasn't smiling at all!

"What's wrong with you two?" Audrey asked.

"Nelson slammed his ears in his front door," Doodle said grimly.

"**I SLAMMED MY EARS IN THE FRONT DOOR!**" yelled Nelson.

"And he can't hear through all the bandages," Doodle added.

"**I CAN'T HEAR *ANYTHING*!**" hollered Nelson.

"That's awful," said Audrey. "How do you talk to each other?"

"It's hard," Doodle sighed. "I use a notepad. He just yells stuff."

"**I CAN'T READ HIS WRITING!**" howled Nelson.

At that moment, Ornela leapt forward, snatched the notepad from Doodle, and began to write furiously. After a few seconds, she held up the notepad and smiled. Audrey could not believe her eyes! Beautifully formed letters spelled out a friendly greeting.

"Boys," Audrey sighed, "meet my cousin."

The boys hit it off with Ornela right away. Nelson was happy to have a new friend with good handwriting. And Doodle was just happy. "How about a game of Hide-N-Seek?" he asked.

"Sure!" said Audrey.

"Sure!" said Ornela.

"HOW ABOUT A GAME OF HIDE-N-SEEK?" yelled Nelson.

The game started out well. Audrey knew all the best places to hide. But to her frustration, Ornela followed her from hiding place to hiding place.

"I'm glad I'm with you," Ornela whispered. "You're the best!"

Audrey wasn't glad. "Find your own hiding place!" she scolded. "You're gonna give me away!"

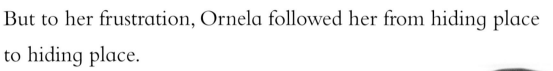

Nelson finally grew tired of Hide-N-Seek
and loudly suggested that they play a guessing game. Everyone agreed.

Audrey started the game by pretending to be a gazelle. She
hopped around the playground gracefully. *Boing! Boing!* It didn't take
long for the others to guess the right answer.

"Gazelle!" they giggled.

When Ornela's turn came, she hopped around the playground just
like Audrey, but no one laughed.

Doodle was puzzled. "Was that a gazelle? Again?" he asked.

"Yes!" said Ornela. She curtsied.

Doodle looked at Audrey. "Is your cousin okay?" he whispered.

"She's fine," Audrey shrugged. "That's just Ornela."

As the days went by, Audrey couldn't go anywhere without her cousin by her side, copying every move she made. Mr. and Mrs. Amaka encouraged Audrey to be patient and to be a good example to Ornela.

"If I had a neck," Audrey grumbled, "that girl would be a royal pain in it!"

As Audrey and Ornela were leaving school on Friday, they met Nelson and Doodle in the hallway.

"Did ya hear?" Doodle asked. "The OssiCone is hosting a talent contest at Village Hall tomorrow night. *Anyone* can enter!"

"DID YOU HEAR ABOUT THE TALENT CONTEST?" Nelson bellowed.

"Is there a prize?" asked Audrey.

"The prize is the best part!" said Doodle. "The winner gets free ice cream for a *whole year!*"

Audrey thought for moment. "This is exciting!" she said finally. "Let's *all* enter!"

"I thought the same thing!" giggled Ornela. "One of us *has* to win!"

The kids talked about the contest for the next few hours. Doodle chose to sing a romantic song. Nelson decided to present a skit about the Easter Bunny. Audrey, however, refused to say what she was planning to do.

"I'm going to keep it a secret until the curtain rises tomorrow night," she announced.

Ornela was very unhappy about Audrey's decision. "Well then..." she mumbled, "mine will be a secret too."

18

From behind the curtain at Village Hall, Audrey watched as her friends and neighbors gathered in. She looked into the sea of faces and felt her stomach start to churn.

"Is anyone out there?" asked Doodle.

"Oh, yes," Audrey said nervously. "The hall is *packed!*"

"You're gonna be great," said Doodle, patting her on the arm.

At that moment, the lights went down and a booming voice filled the hall. "Ladies and gentlemen! Welcome to the First Annual OssiCone Talent Competition!"

As you might expect in such a gathering, the crowd went *wild!*

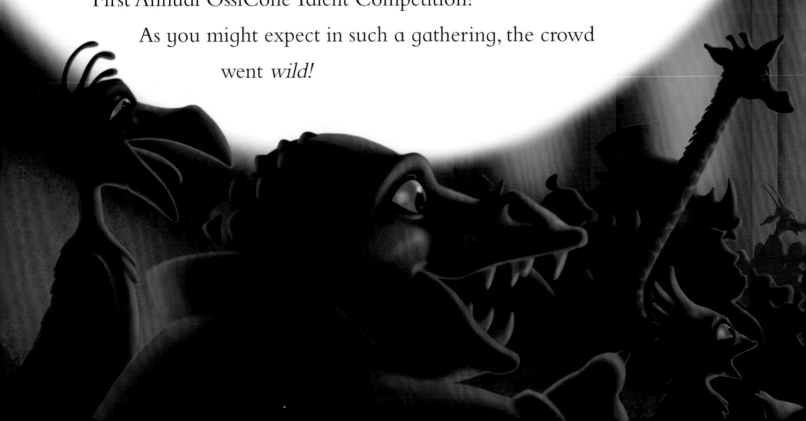

Mr. Weaver kicked off the program by showcasing his old record collection and chirping along with some of his favorite tunes. Everyone enjoyed Mr. Weaver until he started showing pictures of his *entire* family.

Next up was Nelson who entertained the crowd by hopping around the stage, pretending to be the Easter Bunny.

"HIPPITY-HOPPITY, FLIPPITY-FLOPPITY... HERE I COME AGAIN!"

Audrey was relieved when Nelson finished without hurting himself or breaking the eggs in his basket.

Billy Bongo followed Nelson by reading a few jokes he had written. No one except Billy's mother thought the jokes were very funny, but the audience applauded anyway.

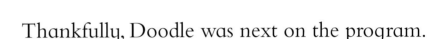

Thankfully, Doodle was next on the program. "My name is Doodle," he told the crowd, "but I'm not good at doodling. Honestly, I'm not good at writing *anything!* So tonight, I will be singing my favorite romantic ballad."

With that, Doodle launched into a sappy rendition of "When I Look At You, Girl." Soon, every woman in the hall was sniffling and swooning.

23

After waiting a long time, Audrey finally heard her name being announced. She tiptoed to center stage and struck a pose. When the lights went up and the curtain rose, a hush fell on Village Hall.

"This evening," Audrey began, "I will recite a poem inspired by the most beautiful place I have ever been. Ladies and gentlemen, I am proud to present 'Lights on Camilla' by M. Herman Bushbaby."

"Hey, that's me!" said a voice from the audience.

As Audrey recited Mr. Bushbaby's poem, everyone sat in silence, captivated by her performance. When she finished, the audience leapt to their feet and applauded heartily. Shouts of *"Bravo!"* and *"Where did you get those shoes?"* filled the air.

Audrey smiled and waved, feeling quite good about herself. But that feeling didn't last very long.

When the curtain dropped and the lights went down, Audrey saw Doodle motioning to her from the shadows.

"She heard you practicing!" he whispered frantically.

"What? Who?" asked Audrey as she walked over to him.

Just as Doodle started to answer, the announcer's voice again filled the hall. "And now... all the way from the Congo... Please make welcome *Ornela Kayembe!*"

Audrey turned to see her cousin waving at her from center stage. Once again, the curtain rose, the lights went up, and the crowd fell silent.

"This evening," Ornela began, "I will recite a poem inspired by a very beautiful place. Ladies and gentlemen, please enjoy another presentation of 'Lights on Camilla' by M. Herman Bushbaby."

26

"Hey, that's me!" said a voice from the audience.

Audrey bristled. *"You've got to be kidding me!"* she growled, barely able to contain her anger.

As Ornela recited the poem, the audience began to snicker. Louder and lounder they laughed until no one could hear what was being said.

"Am I seeing *double*?" cackled a young leopard. "I thought Ornela was an okapi, but maybe she's just a COPY CAT... an OKAPICAT!" The crowd roared with laughter.

Ornela stood very still. Big tears filled her eyes.

As Audrey watched from backstage, she suddenly realized an important thing. *I'm her hero,* she thought. *Ornela is not trying to annoy me or embarrass me. She just needs guidance and lots of love.*

28

Audrey marched out from behind the curtain and joined her cousin in the spotlight. The laughter quickly died down.

"Shame on you!" Audrey said, glaring at the audience. "Nobody deserves to be treated like that. My cousin might want to be like me, but guess what. She's wonderful just like she is!" Audrey put her hand on Ornela's shoulder.

"First of all, she has a kind heart. Second, she is an okapi and okapi's are *gorgeous!* Third, Ornela has a talent that I will *never* have. And, tonight, she's gonna show it to you."

At once, Nelson and Doodle appeared from behind the curtain with a blank chalkboard, a piece of chalk, and a stopwatch.

"Okay, cousin," said Audrey. "You take the chalk. I'll take the clock." Ornela was surprised, but followed Audrey's instructions.

"Ready... set... GO!"

29

Just twenty seconds later, Audrey called "Time's UP!"

When the chalk dust cleared, everyone was amazed to see what Ornela had written. Beautiful letters spelled out a familiar saying:

As the audience cheered, the president of The OssiCone ran to the stage and cleared his throat.

"I have never seen such—such talent!" he said. "Ladies and gentlemen, we have a *WINNER!*" Once again, the crowd went wild.

Ornela squealed with delight. "What am I gonna do with all that ice cream?" she laughed, giving Audrey a big hug.

On Monday afternoon, Ornela boarded the riverboat that would take her home to the Congo.

"Believe it or not," said Audrey, "I wish Ornela didn't have to go!"

"I WISH ORNELA DIDN'T HAVE TO GO!" hollered Nelson.

Audrey looked at Doodle. "I do have one question. Why did Ornela write *your* favorite saying on the chalkboard?"

Doodle grinned. "That's what I was telling her when you were on stage. I found out what she was planning to do and begged her to use her *own* amazing talent. She finally did!"

And so it was that Ornela Kayembe learned that she would never be just like Audrey. But that was okay! Ornela finally found the joy of using her *own* God-given skills.

Meanwhile, Audrey's handwriting did improve, but—better than that—she realized that her actions and attitudes made a big difference to those around her. It's so important to be a good example!

"...we are taking great pains to do what is right, not only in the eyes of the Lord, but also in the eyes of man."

2 CORINTHIANS 8:21

P.S.
The Best thing to do
with ICE CREAM is to
SHARE it !!!

Did you KNOW?

◆   Okapis live in the rainforests of central Africa and are known to be very shy. So shy, in fact, that few people knew about them until they were officially documented in 1890.

◆   The closest relative to the okapi is the giraffe, but with bold stripes on its legs and backside, the okapi appears to be part of the zebra family!

◆   Okapis are **herbivores** (plant-eaters), but they often eat things that a human could never digest—things like charcoal and red clay!

◆   Like giraffes, male okapis have horn-like growths on their heads. They are not *technically* horns; they are **ossicones**! (Does that word sound familiar?)

Did you NOTICE?

*In every Audrey Amaka storybook, you can find at least one tree that is pointing or posing. But did you notice the funky monkey who randomly appears throughout the pages of **this** book? Be sure to look carefully!*